Bear Feels Sick

D0516709

MVFOL

BL: 1.8

AR PTS: 0.5

To Debi, Mark, Addie, and Stephanie:
Dearest family, I hope you always
feel your best. God bless!
—K. W.

To Noah and Levi,
who once made me feel sick,
but now only ever make me feel better.
—J. C.

No part of this publication may be reproduced, stored in a retrieval system,
or transmitted in any form or by any means, electronic, mechanical,
photocopying, recording, or otherwise, without written permission of the publisher.
For information regarding permission, write to Margaret K. McElderry Books,
an imprint of Simon & Schuster Children's Publishing Division,
1230 Avenue of the Americas, New York, NY 10020.

ISBN-13: 978-0-545-10737-2
ISBN-10: 0-545-10737-7

Text copyright © 2007 by Karma Wilson.
Illustrations copyright © 2007 by Jane Chapman. All rights reserved.
Published by Scholastic Inc., 557 Broadway, New York, NY 10012,
by arrangement with Margaret K. McElderry Books, an imprint of
Simon & Schuster Children's Publishing Division. SCHOLASTIC and
associated logos are trademarks and/or registered trademarks of Scholastic Inc.

12 11 10 9 8 7 6 5 4 3 2   8 9 10 11 12 13/0

Printed in the U.S.A.   08
This edition first printing, September 2008

The text for this book is set in Adobe Caslon.
The illustrations for this book are rendered in acrylic paint.

Bear Feels Sick

Karma Wilson

illustrations by Jane Chapman

SCHOLASTIC INC.
New York Toronto London Auckland Sydney
Mexico City New Delhi Hong Kong Buenos Aires

Alone in his cave
as the autumn wind blows,
Bear feels achy
with a stuffed-up nose.

He tosses and he turns,
all huddled in a heap.
Bear feels tired,
but he just can't sleep.

He sniffs and he sneezes.
He whiffs and he wheezes.
And the bear
            feels
                  sick.

His friends gather round.
"Come out, Bear, and play."
Bear shakes his head.
"I'm too sick today."

Mouse mutters, "Oh my,
Bear's head is too hot."
Hare says, "We will help!
Here's a warm, cozy spot."

Bear mumbles and he moans. He grumbles and he groans.

And the bear
feels
sick.

Mouse squeezes Bear tight.
He whispers in his ear,
"It'll be just fine.
Your friends are all here."

Badger fetches water.
Gopher cooks the broth
while Mole soothes Bear
with a cool, wet cloth.

They cover Bear up and he drinks from a cup.

But he still
feels
sick.

Raven says, "*Caw!*
Come along, Owl and Wren.
Let us go gather herbs
to bring back to the den."

They coax Bear to sip
just a smidgen of tea.
"You'll feel better soon,"
says Mouse. "Wait and see."

Bear shakes and he shivers. He coughs and he quivers.

And he still
feels
sick.

The friends fuss and fret.
The friends cook and care.
They keep a close eye
on their poor sick Bear.

They all talk in whispers.
They walk on tippy toes.
They sing lullabies.
Then the bear starts to doze.

They watch Bear for hours.
"We've done all we could."

Then the bear wakes up.

And the bear
feels
GOOD!

Bear cries, "I'm all better.
I'm feeling like new.
I'm not hot and achy.
It's all thanks to you!

"Let's celebrate now.
Let's go out and play.
Let's jump in the leaves.
Let's frolic all day!"

Then Mouse starts to wheeze and Hare starts to sneeze . . .

and the friends
feel
sick!

Bear murmurs, "Don't worry,"
and tucks them in bed.
He bundles them up
and he kisses each head.

He tells all his friends,
"You'll soon feel like new.
You took care of me . . .
   now I'll take care of you."